Druscilla's Halloween

Sally M. Walker

illustrations by Lee White

Carolrhoda Books Minneapolis • New York

Carolrhoda Books
A division of Lerner Publishing Group, Inc.
241 First Avenue North
Minneapolis, MN 55401 U.S.A.

Website address: www.lernerbooks.com

Library of Congress Cataloging-in-Publication Data

Walker, Sally M.
        Druscilla's Halloween / by Sally M. Walker ; illustrated by Lee White.
                        p.   cm.
        Summary: In the time when witches tiptoe about to have their Halloween fun,
ancient Druscilla knows her creaking knees will prevent her from being sneaky and sets
out to find a silent conveyance for herself, her cat, and her jack o' lantern.
        ISBN: 978-0-8225-8941-9 (lib. bdg. : alk. paper)
        [1. Witches—Fiction. 2. Old age—Fiction. 3. Halloween—Fiction.]
        I. White, Lee, 1970- ill. II. Title.
        PZ7.W153845Dru 2009
        [E]—dc22   2008041163

Manufactured in the United States of America
1 2 3 4 5 6 - DP - 14 13 12 11 10 09

In memory of Nancy Peterson—
Librarian, first reader, friend
—S. m. w.

to Gene, Ken, and Machiko
—l. w.

Once upon a HALLOWEEN,
a million spells ago,

witches prepared for a spine-chilling night. They scooped out pumpkins and carved scary faces.

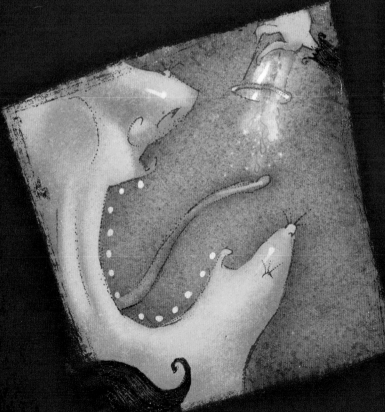

They gulped potions that grew extra warts on their chins.

While their cats practiced hissing, the witches honed their cackling skills, with petrifying results. Last but not least, they moussed the hair on each cat's back, so it stood up spikier than ever.

In those days, witches sneaked silently on foot,
spooking and spelling. So before they crept toward the
townfolks' homes, they practiced walking on tiptoe.

All of them but ancient Druscilla, the ricketiest witch of all. She slumped on the floor of her mountaintop house, moaning as loudly as the wind in the trees.

"Woe is me. What shall I do?" Druscilla wailed to the rafters. She slapped her knees angrily and stood up.

SNAP!

CRACK!

Druscilla covered her ears.
"Hush, you treacherous old knees.

You're robbing me of the element of surprise."

She limped to the door and glared down at the town. Her cat Drizzle wound himself around her legs. "I must think fast. I won't let noisy knees spoil my plans."

WELCOME

SNAP! CRACK! CREAK! POP!

An earsplitting HEEEE-HAW pierced the air. Druscilla grabbed her jack o' lantern and a rope. With eyes like steel, she said, "Come now, Drizzle. I have an idea." Druscilla shambled out to the field.

SNAP! CRACK! CREAK! POP!

field

Her uproarious knees sent
squirrels scurrying into the trees.
Rabbits dove into their holes.
Fireflies turned off their lights.

Druscilla's donkey rolled his eyes.

Druscilla tied the rope around his neck.

Carefully balancing her jack o' lantern, she pulled herself up onto the donkey's back. She cackled triumphantly.

"Come, Drizzle. We have work to do. Giddyup!"

The donkey didn't budge.

Druscilla kicked her heels.
Nothing. She kicked some
more. He still didn't move.

She squeezed her eyes shut,
pinched her nose tightly and
forced herself to add, "Please?"
Still no luck.

"Okay, pal. You asked for it."
She closed her eyes and chanted,
*"Swiftly, silently gallop I say,
Carry me quickly to town today!"*

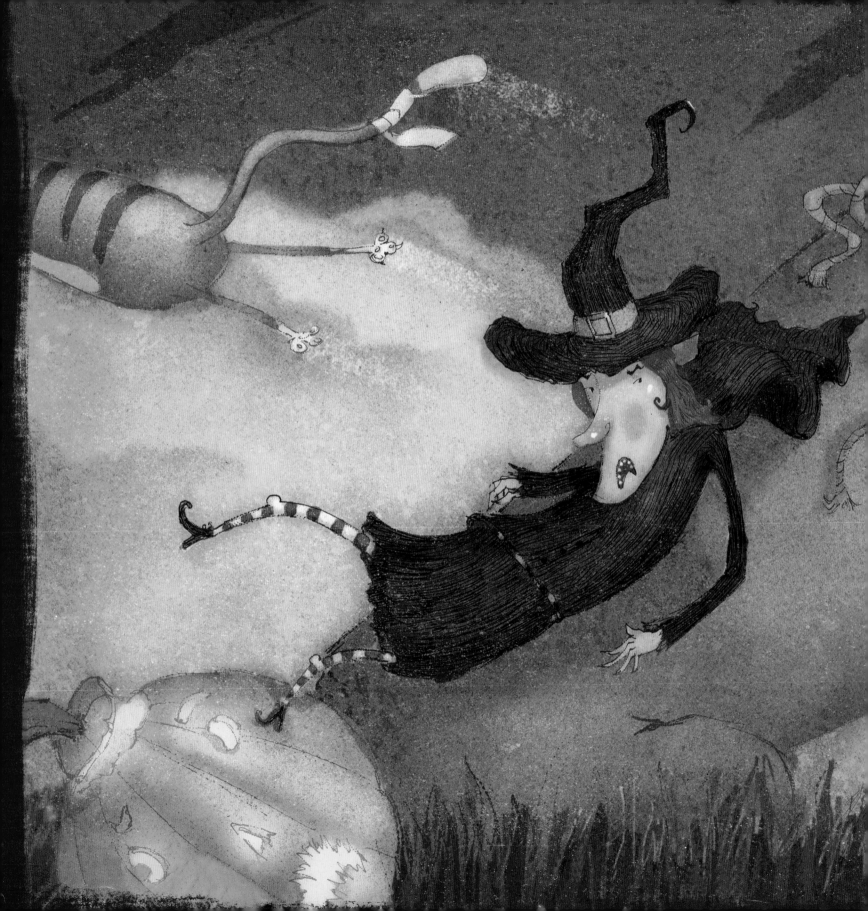

But the donkey was too stubborn to fall under Druscilla's spell. He brayed again and sat down. Drizzle leaped as the jack o' lantern rolled. Druscilla slid to the ground with a groan.

Druscilla struggled to her feet.

SNAP! CRACK! CREAK! POP!

The noises bent the blades of grass and echoed off the hills.

But Druscilla
smiled when she
saw her wheelbarrow.
With an o-o-o-f that came
all the way from her toes, she
heaved herself and her jack o' lantern
in. Drizzle settled on her lap. Druscilla
closed her eyes and chanted,
   "Swiftly, silently wheelbarrow roll,
   Soon my spells will take their toll."
The wheelbarrow rolled downhill, zigzagging wildly.
Before Druscilla could chant a stopping spell . . .

Spitting mad, Druscilla
shook her fist at the town.
"Don't count me out! I have
not yet begun to fright!"
Druscilla hobbled homeward.

SNAP! CRACK! CREAK! POP!

When her chickens heard her
coming, they shivered so hard their
feathers fell off. The wind swirled
them up around Druscilla. She
smiled another witchy smile.
Quickly, Druscilla took off her
cape and filled it with feathers.
"Drizzle, we have work to do."

Druscilla smeared her arms
with paste. She patted feathers
onto them until her arms were
covered from shoulder to fingertip.
Druscilla cackled and flapped her
arms. She rose to the kitchen
ceiling. Circling once, she kicked
open the door and flew outside to
try her wings.

Her cries of success turned to tears when a dark cloud burst and rain soaked her chickeny wings. A downpour of feathers fell to the ground as the rain washed away the paste. Druscilla landed just in time.

"Even if the wings had worked, there would have been no seat for you. But we can't give up now," she told Drizzle.

Leftover feathers dotted the kitchen floor. Druscilla shook her head and picked up her broom. Just as she swept her first sweep, she thought an interesting thought.

Druscilla closed her eyes and chanted:
"Eye of toad, tail of bat,
A fine, flat place to seat my cat.
Handle thin, handle long,
Perfect to hang my pumpkin on.
Blood of worms, wings of bees,
A quiet flight for noisy knees.
Up and down, around the room
Get up and fly, you beautiful broom!"

The broom rose into the air. It hovered, waiting, in front of Druscilla.

"Drizzle, it's
time we were
swept off
our feet!"

Druscilla
grabbed her
emergency back-
up jack o' lantern
and hung it from
the handle. She perched
herself behind it. Drizzle
leaped on and growled a happy growl.

Before you could say whoosh, they whisked out the door.

The rest is history.

Inventor
Flying Broomstick

Druscilla

Druscilla's silent ambush became a witchy legend. That long-ago Halloween night, Druscilla successfully scared each child—only as much as he or she wanted to be scared—just as she had planned.

And at the next worldwide witch council,
the witches took a vote:

Tiptoe vs. Broomsticks.
BROOMSTICKS WON BY A LANDSLIDE.